Acknowledgements

Thank you to my family and friends for providing the inspiration for my characters and stories.

A very special thank you to my son, Jason, for his photography skills and apologies for the embarrassment I caused him whilst taking the photos of Barra Bear and Carly Cat, we did get some funny looks and comments!

Thanks also to Richard and Kevin at For The Right Reasons for their help in producing this book.

Email <u>barraandcarly@btinternet.com</u>

Facebook <u>barrabear.carlycat@facebook.com</u>

Twitter@BarraAndCarly

ISBN: 978-1-910205-05-1

"MISSION POSSIBLE!"

The telephone rang "tring, tring."

"Hello, Barra Bear speaking, how can I help you."

A mysterious voice at the other end of the line replied "Your mission, should you choose to accept it, is to bring lots of smiles to everyone, every day. Are you prepared to take up this challenge? You know what you must do, Barra, good luck."

A WEE TRIP TO FORT GEORGE

Barra Bear and Carly Cat are the best of friends. They live very happily with Lady M of Balloch, His Lordship Mr Grumpy Pants, their lovely son Mr J and their family of wonderfully kind bears but, now and again, Barra and Carly like to go out on little adventures and have a wee bit of fun.

"Well Carly, where would you like to visit today?" asked Barra.

"There are so many lovely places around here, you choose Barra" said Carly.

"How about Fort George, we haven't been there before?" said Barra.

"Excellent idea Barra" said Carly. "Let's get going".

Barra and Carly got ready and off they went to catch the bus to Fort George. It was a beautiful, sunny day, just ideal for a wee trip.

Once they reached Fort George, Barra and Carly visited the new Highlander Museum and had a long walk round the Fort, taking in the lovely views around the Moray Firth over to Inverness and the Black Isle.

"Oh look", said Barra, "there's a boat out in the Firth, I think it's one of those Dolphin Cruise Boats. I would like to go on one of those". "Me too" said Carly, "we will have to do that one day soon".

They saw some soldiers out on parade, they were very good at marching. Barra and Carly tried to join in but they just couldn't get their arms and legs to work at the same time as the soldiers. "This is really hard" said Barra. "It certainly is" said Carly, "I think we will leave the marching to the soldiers", she laughed.

There were lots of interesting things to see and they read all about the history of the Fort.

"Ooh, I'm a bit hungry and thirsty after all that exercise" said Barra. "Shall we find the café and have a cup of tea?"

"What a good idea" said Carly, "I have heard that they have lovely cakes there".

Barra and Carly went in search of the café and once they found it they were very pleased to see that it did indeed have lovely cakes.

"Two cups of tea and two of your splendid strawberry tarts please" Barra asked the friendly Chef. "Certainly Sir" said the Chef. "Please take a seat and I will bring them over to you".

"Thank you very much" said Barra and he and Carly chose a table on the patio where they could sit in the sunshine.

The strawberry tarts were absolutely delicious and went down a treat. "Thank you Mr Chef" said Barra and Carly, "We so enjoyed those wonderful strawberry tarts".

"Strawberry Tarts are my speciality" said the Chef, "I am so pleased that you enjoyed them so much. Hope to see you both again soon."

"Well, we had better go and catch the bus back home now" said Barra, "Lady M will be wondering where we are".

Barra and Carly set off for the bus stop and soon they were home. They told the bears all about their lovely day out and the bears did laugh when Barra told them about their attempts at marching.

Barra and Carly showed everyone a nice picture of them sitting at the Fort near the drawbridge.

"We read about an event that takes place at Fort George in the Summer called "The Celebration of the Centuries" said Barra. "It sounds very interesting and we should all have another day out to Fort George when that is on, it would be such good fun".

"Yes, Yes, Yes!" shouted everyone, "and we can get to try some of Mr Chef's wonderful strawberry tarts as well."

"I am so tired" said Carly, yawning. "Me too" said Barra, "it's all that fresh air and the marching really tired me out. Time for bed, I think".

"I so enjoyed our wee trip" said Carly. "So did I" said Barra. Then they both fell fast asleep dreaming of their day out and all the other lovely places they could visit for their next adventure.

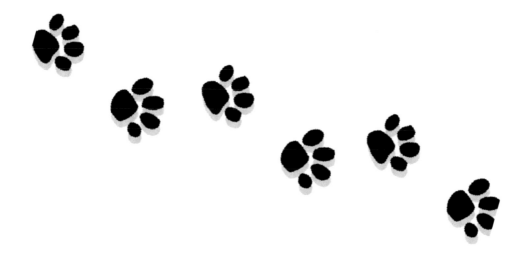

A WEE TRIP TO THE NESS ISLANDS

"Good Morning Carly" said Barra, "how are you this fine sunny morning?".

"Just grand." said Carly. "Do you fancy a wee day out for a nice walk round the Ness Islands?"

"I do indeed." said Barra. "Let's not waste the day then, let's get organized and go and catch the bus into town".

Barra and Carly set off and when they arrived in town, they walked along the riverside to The Islands. First they went to have a wee paddle at the mini beach under the bridge. "Oh the water is so cold", said Carly, dipping her toes in the water, gingerly. "No its not" shouted Barra, "come on in, don't be such a scaredy cat, Carly!"

They splashed about in the water for ages, then they set off to explore the paths through the Islands. "There used to be a roller skating rink here a long time ago" said Barra, I think it was over there in the middle." "How do you know that?" asked Carly. "I once heard Lady M talking about it, she used to go there when she was young". "That must have been a VERY, VERY long time ago then!" shrieked Carly, laughing loudly.

"There's some fishermen over there" said Barra. "Do you want to go over to watch and see if they catch anything." "I've never seen anyone fishing before." said Carly "Let's go then".

They ran over the bridges to the other side of the river and down on to the stonies.

"We need to be very quiet or we will scare the fish away" said Barra. They watched the fishermen, quietly and intently. Soon they could see that one of the fishermen had indeed caught a fish. Barra and Carly watched him reel in the fish very carefully. "Good catch" said Barra as the fisherman walked back to the fishermens' hut.

"Good afternoon", said the fisherman, "did you enjoy watching us fishing? "We certainly did", said Barra and Carly together. "I've never seen anyone fishing before" said Carly, "it was very interesting. Will you have your fish for your dinner tonight?" "Yes, Mrs Maxwell, will cook it for us, she is a very good chef. There is nothing better than freshly caught fish, it is just delicious, my mouth is watering just thinking about it."

Mr Maxwell asked Barra and Carly if they would like a cup of tea and a piece of Mrs Maxwell's homemade Victoria Sponge. "Mrs Maxwell always gives me a big flask of tea and lots of cake for all the fishermen, there is plenty for everyone". "Ooh, yes please", said Barra and Carly and they sat down with the fishermen to have their tea and cake.

"That was so yummy" said Barra. "Mmm, it sure was." said Carly, "Do pass on our thanks to Mrs Maxwell, that truly was a splendiferous cake."

Barra and Carly said goodbye to the fishermen and set off to get the bus home. "Enjoy your fish" shouted Barra as they headed back along the riverside. "Thanks, I will" said Mr Maxwell, "do come and visit us again soon."

When Barra and Carly got home they told the bears all about their lovely day and how exciting it was to see the fishermen catch a fish. They showed the bears a lovely picture of them sitting on the stonies at the River Ness, with the Ness Islands in the background.

The bears all agreed it was a lovely picture. Barra told them about the Roller Skating Rink that used to be in the Islands and they did have a good laugh picturing Lady M trying to roller skate.

They laughed and laughed and laughed so much that Lady M came to ask them what was so funny but, strangely enough, nobody told her!

A WEE BOAT TRIP ON THE MORAY FIRTH

"What a lovely day it is" said Barra, stretching all his body out and doing his wake up exercises. "I think we should go on that Dolphin Cruise we were talking about last night. What do you think Carly?

"That sounds like a very good idea" said Carly. "Where do you catch the boat, Barra?" asked Carly. "Down at the Marina, I think. I'm sure the bus driver can take us to the right place. Come on then, let's get going, don't dilly dally, Carly." They were soon ready and off they set to catch the bus.

"Two tickets to the Marina", Mr Driver, said Barra. "Where are you two heading today then Barra", asked the bus driver, "Dolphin Cruise, is it?". "Spot on" said Barra, "have you been on one before". "No, I haven't but I would like to one of these days. Will you tell me all about it on the way home?" asked the bus driver. "Of course we will" said Carly, "I am so looking forward to it".

When they arrived at the Marina, they followed the signs to the Dolphin Cruises and boarded the boat with the other passengers. There was a group of Chinese tourists on board and they chattered away non-stop, taking photographs of absolutely everything, including Barra and Carly. "Those Chinese are very friendly aren't they Barra" said Carly, "I do wish I knew what they were saying, it would be nice to chat with them." "Don't worry, Carly", said Barra, even though we don't understand what they are saying, we can see that they are having a brilliant time and that's all that matters."

They sailed out of the Marina, under the Kessock Bridge, past Kilmuir, Avoch and Rosemarkie and headed out to Chanonry Point at Fortrose, the best place to spot the dolphins.

"Look over there Carly" shouted Barra, "there's Fort George, remember when we visited there and we could see Rosemarkie and Fortrose from that side of the Firth." "Yes, that was such a good day out Barra", said Carly "and I am enjoying today's trip just as much."

"Look, everyone, said the Captain, if you watch just over there, you will see some dolphins swimming by".   Everyone watched intently, the Chinese tourists with their cameras at the ready and, sure enough, a pod of dolphins could be seen, jumping and splashing through the water. "They are absolutely beautiful" said Carly "and they look so happy, having lots of fun with their friends."   Snap, snap, snap went the Chinese tourists, taking hundreds of photos.   "Well, they will certainly have at least one excellent picture, the amount they have taken" laughed Barra.

The Captain announced that tea and shortbread would now be served whilst they continued to watch the dolphins.   The dolphins swum back and fore, playing to the crowd, they really did look like they were putting on a show for everyone.   "Mmm, lovely shortbread Carly" said Barra. "It certainly is", said Carly, grabbing another piece for each of them, before the Chinese tourists ate the rest.   "I think they like eating shortbread as much as taking photos", laughed Carly.

Soon they headed back to the Marina and as Barra and Carly disembarked they thanked the Captain for the lovely boat trip.   The Chinese tourists also thanked the Captain, many, many times, at least Barra and Carly thought that was what they were saying.

Barra and Carly waited for the Balloch bus and when it arrived they were pleased to see that it was the same bus driver who had dropped them off earlier. "Oh good," said Barra, "we can tell Mr Driver all about the Dolphin Cruise".

Barra and Carly climbed aboard the bus and told the bus driver how much they had enjoyed the Dolphin Cruise "You really will have to go on a Dolphin Cruise" said Carly "it was so much fun".   "I will make sure that I go soon" said the bus driver, "thank you so much for telling me all about it". "Barra and Carly, that's your stop now" shouted the bus driver and they jumped off the bus and ran home up the hill to tell the bears all about their lovely day out.

They showed the bears a picture of themselves at the Marina, looking out over the Moray Firth and the Kessock Bridge over to the Black Isle which one of the Chinese tourists had taken for them.

"What a lovely picture" chorused all the bears at once. "Those Chinese tourists do take a good photo." "And so they should," said Barra, "they took hundreds and hundreds of photos!"

"Well time for bed everyone" said Barra, and Barra and Carly fell fast asleep, dreaming of splashing dolphins and what adventures they could get up to tomorrow.

A WEE TRIP TO URQUHART CASTLE

Barra and Carly had just had their breakfast and were thinking about what they could do today.

"Carly, it's your turn to choose where to go today, where would you like to go?" said Barra.

"What about Urquhart Castle, Barra, I believe it is quite an interesting place to visit. People come from all over the world to visit it and we only live up the road and have never been." "Right, Urquhart Castle it is then." said Barra.

Off they set to catch the Loch Ness Tourist Trail Bus and they decided to pretend they were foreign visitors for the day. "Where shall we pretend to be from?" Carly asked Barra. "How about New York?" suggested Barra, I'm quite good at an American accent." "Good idea", said Carly, "this is going to be such fun."

Barra and Carly boarded the bus along with the other tourists and the bus driver told them all about the legend of Nessie, the Loch Ness Monster, as they drove along the loch side on their way to Urquhart Castle.

When they arrived, they went into the Visitor Centre and headed down the steps into the castle grounds. "Wow", said Barra, "this is like an underground cave, it's like something out of a James Bond film, very impressive, and we haven't even reached the Castle yet".

They walked over the drawbridge and into the castle. There were lots of steep steps to climb and once they reached the top they took in the views of Loch Ness. "Oh look there's a boat on the Loch" said Carly. "I think that's one of the cruise boats that go looking for Nessie" said Barra.

"Would you like to go on a Nessie cruise one day Carly?" asked Barra. "Oh yes, I think that would be very exciting. Do you really think we would see Nessie, Barra, I might be a bit scared if we did" said Carly.

Barra laughed and said "You are such a scaredy cat, Carly. Nessie is a very friendly little monster and she wouldn't hurt anyone, she likes people coming to look for her and she loves to play hide and seek. She is very good at it and that's why not many people have actually seen her. "If you are really sure then Barra, I think I would like to go on a Nessie cruise one day". "Good", said Barra, "then we shall".

Barra and Carly followed the rest of the tourists to the café for afternoon tea and they so enjoyed the lovely cream buns.

The bus driver tooted his horn to let everyone know it was time to leave and they all climbed aboard for the journey back to Inverness.

Barra and Carly said goodbye to the bus driver and the other tourists and jumped on the bus home to Balloch.

"Do you think everybody believed we were Americans today?" asked Barra, still in his New York accent. "I'm sure they did" said Carly, "I think we did really well keeping it up all day" and they laughed all the way home.

When Barra and Carly got home they told the bears all about their day out, still in their best American accents. The bears thought this was a hilarious prank and said they would have believed they were American too if they didn't know they were really from Balloch.

Barra and Carly showed the bears a picture that the bus driver had taken of them with Urquhart Castle and Loch Ness in the background.

"What a lovely day that was" said Carly "but gosh, I'm tired now". "Me too", said Barra. We really must go on that Nessie cruise soon".
And dreaming of that, they were soon fast asleep.

A WEE TRIP TO NAIRN BEACH

It was another lovely day and Barra and Carly thought it was time for another wee day out.

"Your turn to choose for today's trip" said Barra "Where do you fancy?"

"What about Nairn Beach, I do like to feel the sand between my toes and have a paddle in the sea" said Carly.

"Right, Nairn Beach it is, come on then, let's get going, we will need our buckets and spades for building sandcastles" said Barra.

Barra and Carly set off to the bus stop and were soon on their way. When they arrived at Nairn, they wondered what to do first.

"Shall we have a game of putting, a walk along the links, a paddle in the sea, build sandcastles, have a cup of tea or have an ice cream?" asked Barra.

"So many choices." said Carly. There is so much to do in Nairn, I love coming here. Let's have a game of putting first before we head to the beach."

Now, Barra was very competitive when it came to sports but Carly just liked to play for fun. "Whoever loses the putting challenge can buy the afternoon tea" said Barra convinced he would win. Carly laughed and agreed, thinking to herself, he doesn't remember that I won the last time, ha, ha, ha. It was a very close match but Carly won by 3 shots, cheering "Yes!" as she sunk her last putt.

Barra was a wee bit grumpy after his defeat but he didn't stay grumpy for long as Carly is such a caring little cat that she gave him a big hug and said "Come on Mr Grumpy Pants, you can be so like His Lordship at times. Let's go and have some fun, I'll treat you to the afternoon tea, but first let's go and have a paddle and build sandcastles".

Barra and Carly headed down to the beach and went paddling, jumping over the waves, as they crashed towards the beach. They laughed and laughed and laughed, they were having so much fun. Then they built a fantastic sandcastle, digging out round the edges to make a moat, it looked most impressive and they were very pleased with their efforts.

"It's such a shame that the tide will come in and wash it away soon" said Barra. "That's part of the fun" said Carly, "you have to come back again to build another one". "That's very true" said Barra.

"Let's go and have that afternoon tea now" said Barra "I'm so hungry and thirsty. Let's go to the little café up at the Links".

"Super idea, I wonder if they will have lovely cakes like the café at Fort George" said Carly. "I'm sure they will," said Barra "come on, hurry up, I really am very, very hungry". They ran up the beach in their bare feet as fast as they could to the café.

"Good afternoon" said Barra and Carly to the lovely, friendly girl in the cafe, "We would like two teas and two of your lovely cream scones, please. "Certainly sir and ma'am" said the girl, whose name was Merina, it said so on her name badge. "Please choose a table and I will bring them over to you".

"Thank you very much Merina," said Barra and Carly. "We will sit at the outside tables as it is such a nice day" said Barra.

Merina brought Barra and Carly their tea and scones which were absolutely delicious. "Compliments to the chef," said Barra as they said goodbye to Merina. "His scones were truly scrumptious, we will visit again soon for some more."

"Time to go home now, I think Carly," said Barra as they reluctantly headed off to catch the bus home. Lady M will be wondering where we are.

When they got home, they told the bears all about their adventures of the day, Carly did laugh when she told them that she had beaten Barra in the putting match. "Well done you!" shouted everyone.

Barra and Carly showed everyone a picture of them at the beach looking over the Moray Firth and they all thought it was a beautiful view.

"Don't you think I'm getting quite good at doing these timed photos Carly," said Barra. "You have to be quite quick to pose but I must admit they are rather good" said Carly.

"I so enjoyed our day out at Nairn" said Carly. "Me too" said Barra, "we will have to go back again soon".

Barra and Carly both started yawning at the same time. "Time for bed" they said and they both fell fast asleep, their little legs twitching, as they dreamed of jumping over the waves and even more adventures to come.

A WEE TRIP TO INVERGORDON

Barra and Carly had just wakened up, had a good stretch and wondered what they would do today.

"Did you hear Lady M say last night that she was going to visit her friend Mrs MacLeod in Invergordon today?" said Barra. "I did indeed" said Carly, "I wonder if she would take us with her. There may be one of those big cruise ships in for us to have a look at." "Let's go and ask her then" said Barra.

"Lady M, can we please, please, please come with you to Invergordon today, we haven't been out for a few days and we fancy a wee run in the car." said Barra. "Of course you can" said Lady M, "let's go and ask His Lordship Mr Grumpy Pants if he wants to come too, he might even take the posh car out for the day".

"Your Lordship" shouted Barra, "do you want to come with us to Invergordon today". "Oh alright then" said His Lordship, a bit grumpily, as usual, "I suppose I don't have much to do today. I think I will take the posh car out today and give it a wee day out as well."

"Hurray!" shouted Barra and Carly together, we do love going in the posh car." "I feel just like the Queen" said Carly.

Barra and Carly raced to the car, climbed in and put on their seat belts. "Everybody happy" said Lady M "Yes thank you" said Barra and Carly and off they went.

Barra and Carly looked at all the lovely views on the way, over the Kessock Bridge, up the hill at Tore, down the hill at the other side to the Cromarty Bridge and along by the Cromarty Firth to Invergordon.

"I wonder if we will see a big boat" said Carly "I would love to go travelling on one of those." "We may be lucky, let's hope so" said Barra.

They reached Invergordon and Barra and Carly were disappointed to see there were no boats at the quayside. "Look, look," shouted Barra " there's an oil rig over there, wow, it is so big." Barra and Carly asked His Lordship if they could stop to have a look at the oil rig. "Let's take Lady M to Mrs MacLeod's house first and then we can come back and have a wee walk and a closer look at the rig. Lady M will blether for ages to Mrs MacLeod and we will be so bored, oil rigs are much more interesting."

His Lordship delivered Lady M safely to Mrs MacLeod's and said "I'll be back in an hour, don't blether too long please." Then His Lordship, Barra and Carly went back to see the oil rig.

His Lordship had worked on an oil rig a long time ago and he knew lots about them. They saw that there was a name on the rig, "Galaxy 1". His Lordship told them that all the oil rigs had special names.

"If that rig is called Galaxy 1, does that mean it can go into space?" asked Carly, "that's where a galaxy is, isn't it?" Carly had made His Lordship laugh, a rare occurrence! "No Carly, unfortunately not" said His Lordship, "only rockets and spaceships can go into space."

"Well," said Barra," I bet that nice Mr Brian Cox, the scientist on the telly box, could easily make some rockets and send Galaxy 1 into space." His Lordship laughed again, twice in one day, extremely rare! "No doubt, he could" said his Lordship. Barra, Carly and His Lordship had a good look around Galaxy 1 and watched the crane lifting things on to the rig. "We had better head back to collect Lady M now" said His Lordship, "although I'm sure she will still be blethering."

They arrived at Mrs MacLeod's and His Lordship beeped the car horn very loudly, Lady M got the message loud and clear. She waved goodbye to Mrs MacLeod as she got into the car. "See you again soon" shouted Lady M.

"Can we stop at Foulis for a cup of tea on the way home and I will treat you all to a nice cake" said Lady M.   "Ooh, yes please," said everyone.

They could not believe their eyes when they arrived at the restaurant at Foulis. "Look at the size of those meringues, they are enormous, I have to have one of those, please, please, please," said Barra.   "I think we should share," said Lady M, "nobody could eat a whole one!" "I bet I could" said His Lordship. "No doubt, YOU can" said Lady M, you have a bottomless pit for a stomach."   They ordered 3 meringues and a large pot of tea and sat by the window to watch the seals basking on the sandbank in the Cromarty Firth.

Barra, Carly and Lady M had ½ a meringue each and His Lordship managed to eat 1 ½ all by himself.   "Mmm, that was really good" said everyone.   "Time for home now, Mr J will be home from school soon. It's a shame, he couldn't come with us today, he would have loved one of those meringues" said Lady M.

When they arrived home, Barra and Carly told the bears all about their day out and how His Lordship had enjoyed the trip as well.   Today he had been really quite ungrumpy, most unusual.

They told the bears all about the oil rig and how it was called Galaxy 1 and showed them a picture of themselves with the oil rig which His Lordship had taken. Barra and Carly told the bears all the things His Lordship had told them about the oil rig and they were very impressed at how they had remembered so much.

McKellar Tweed was a very clever bear and he had read about oil rigs in a book but he said it was far more interesting to hear about them from Barra and Carly.

His Lordship had told Barra and Carly that it was very cold on the oil rigs and the bears all agreed that they loved their cosy home at Balloch and would not like to live on an oil rig.

Barra and Carly were very tired after all the fresh air today and were soon nodding off to sleep. "I wonder if we should write to Mr Brian, the scientist, to ask him to make some rockets to send Galaxy 1 into space with us and all the bears on board. We would even invite Mr Brian to come with us, he is so handsome" murmured Carly. They soon fell fast asleep, dreaming of spaceships, the moon and the stars, what an adventure that would be.

A WEE TRIP FOR AFTERNOON TEA
AT CULLODEN HOUSE

Barra and Carly had a long lie this morning because they were a bit tired as they had been going on so many days out.

"What shall we do today Barra?" asked Carly. "Is there somewhere near we can visit today? "Let me think," said Barra, "how about Culloden House? We pass by it most days but I have never been inside and I believe they do nice afternoon teas." "That will do nicely" said Carly. "Mr Michael from up the road is the chef at Culloden House, we must go and sample his cakes. Let's go for a little walk first to work up an appetite."

"Great idea," said Barra and off they set, heading up the hill at Balloch to the woods.

There was a woodland trail to follow which would take them through the woods to Culloden and along the paths where the wood carvings were to Culloden House. Barra and Carly wandered through the woods, listening to the birds tweeting, kicking up the leaves as they walked. They found a stream and jumped back and fore over it, then paddled in the water, looking for frogs. "There's one there!" shouted Barra. "So it is" said Carly, just spotting it before it jumped away. "This is such good fun, isn't it" said Carly.

After all that running about Barra and Carly were really looking forward to their afternoon tea and they set off to Culloden House.
They walked along the Gruffalo path, looking at the lovely wood carvings which Mr Ian had made, they were so good. "That Mr Ian is a very clever man to make these, I read in the paper that he carves them with a chainsaw" said Barra. "Really" said Carly, "that must be so dangerous, we better not try that then!" "Definitely not!" exclaimed Barra.

Barra and Carly arrived at the gate at Culloden House and they decided that Culloden House was indeed a splendid building.

They walked up the extremely long driveway and up the red carpeted steps. "The staff must have known we were coming today" said Barra, they have put the red carpet out for us". "Is that really for us Barra?" asked Carly. "Of course it is" said Barra, "Many very important people come to stay at Culloden House. I believe Elton John has stayed here." "Really," said Carly, "I do love his music, do you think he will he here today? I would love to meet some famous people." "Elton will probably be on tour somewhere with his red piano, I'm sure" said Barra, "he works very hard you know."

Barra and Carly were welcomed by the concierge who showed them into the lounge and they ordered their afternoon tea. Mr Michael, the chef, had seen Barra and Carly walking up the driveway and he brought their afternoon tea to them personally.

"Good afternoon Barra and Carly" said Mr Michael, "thank you for coming to see us at Culloden House, I do hope you enjoy your afternoon tea. I have put extra filling in your sandwiches and lots of extra jam and cream on the scones just for you, as you are such very important guests."

"As important as Elton John?" asked Carly. "Even more important" replied Mr Michael, "you and Barra are the most important guests we have ever had!" They all laughed and Barra and Carly tucked into their sandwiches and cakes.

"That was the best ever afternoon tea we have ever had" said Barra, my seams are fit to burst." "Me too" said Carly, "it was so yummy. Mr Michael certainly is the best cake maker ever!"

Barra and Carly shared the last cake, said thank you to Mr Michael and walked home the long way round to work off some of the feast they had just eaten.

When they arrived home they told the bears all about their walk through the woods and their wonderful afternoon tea. "Mr Michael told us that we were the most important guests that had ever visited Culloden House" said Carly. The bears were suitably impressed and they all agreed that they were very honoured indeed to have such important people as Barra and Carly as their friends.

They showed the bears a picture of them sitting on the lawn at Culloden House which Mr Michael had kindly taken for them.

"What a splendid house" said the bears, "wouldn't it be nice to live there, so much space to run around and play hide and seek. Even better, we would have Mr Michael to make lovely cakes for us, mmm, that would be the best bit of all."

Barra and Carly rubbed their full tummies and agreed that living at Culloden House would be wonderful but they would miss Lady M, His Lordship Mr Grumpy Pants and most of all Mr J, so they decided they would be quite happy to stay put at Wellside.

"Time for bed" sighed Barra, "it has been another good day Carly." "It certainly has Barra," whispered Carly, as she nodded off to sleep, Nighty, night" said Barra and soon they were both fast asleep.

A WEE TRIP ON A NESSIE CRUISE

"Good Morning Barra" said Carly "Do you remember when we were at Urquhart Castle, we saw a Nessie Cruise boat on Loch Ness?"

"Good morning to you too Carly" said Barra. "Yes I do indeed remember. You must have been reading my mind, I've just been thinking that we could perhaps go on a Nessie Cruise today."

"That's really weird that we were thinking the same" said Carly. "That's the decision made then, that's what we shall do today."

Barra and Carly got organized and set off to catch the bus to the Caledonian Canal where the Nessie Cruises set off from.

When they arrived at the Canal, there was a big boat going through the locks so they stopped to watch. "Wow, look at all that water, isn't it amazing how these locks work, it's like the boat is going down big watery steps, one at a time.   The person who invented these locks must have been, very, very clever." said Carly.   "It was a gentleman called Thomas Telford who designed the Caledonian Canal" said Barra, "I read about him in one of Lady M's books. I agree with you, Mr Telford was a very clever man."

Once the boat had completed its journey through all the locks, Barra and Carly boarded the Nessie Cruise boat and the boat set off to Loch Ness. They waved to everybody they saw as they travelled along the canal and they were so pleased that everybody smiled and waved back at them.

Soon they reached Dochgarroch and the water became so much wider as the River Ness and the Canal joined together. "I'm not too sure about this boat cruise now" said Carly, "dry land looks very far away." "Wait until you get out on Loch Ness," said Barra "it will be even further away!" "Oh no" said Carly "I think I'm going to be a wee bit frightened."   "No you won't," said Barra, "you know I will look after you. I'm sure you will really enjoy yourself."

They arrived at Lochend and sailed into the Loch, there was so much water and Carly held on tightly to Barra's paw.

"Right Carly, get your binoculars out, time to do some Nessie spotting." Barra and Carly were so intent on looking for Nessie that Carly completely forgot that she had been a bit scared of all the water.   "Barra, do you think we will see Nessie today?" asked Carly. "You never know" replied Barra, "she only comes out for very special people, keep looking and you just might see her".   "Barra, Barra," shouted Carly, "look over there, I'm sure I saw Nessie peeping out of the water just over there." Barra looked through his binoculars over to where Carly was pointing and shouted "It is, it is, Carly, well spotted, get a photo, quick."   But, by the time, Carly snapped the shot, Nessie had disappeared again. "She's at that Hide and Seek again, Barra, remember you told me how good she was at that game." "That's right but, keep your eyes peeled and you may see her again." said Barra.

The boat sailed all the way up to Urquhart Castle and whilst they were sailing, the girls served a lovely afternoon tea with scones, shortbread and cakes.   Carly was really enjoying the cruise now, tea and cakes make everything OK.

They didn't see Nessie again whilst they were sailing back to Inverness but, Barra said that Nessie must have thought that he and Carly were very special to have let them see her even once.

When they arrived back at the locks, Barra and Carly thanked the Captain of the Nessie Cruise boat and they jumped on the bus back home to Balloch.

Barra and Carly arrived home and ran into the house shouting "We've seen Nessie, we've seen Nessie!" "Do you have a picture of Nessie then?" asked the bears. "Unfortunately not", said Barra, "she swam away before we could get a picture." We do have a nice picture at the locks at the Caledonian Canal, would you like to see that one?" asked Barra. "Well, I suppose that will have to do then, although we really would have liked to see a picture of Nessie" grumbled the bears.

The bears still didn't believe that Barra and Carly had really seen Nessie. "Nobody sees Nessie, it's just a legend" said McKellar Tweed, the wisest and cleverest of the bears. "Well we both did" said Barra and Carly together. "You must be very, very, very special indeed then" said McKellar Tweed. "You must remember this day forever".

"We will never, ever forget it" said Barra. "We certainly will not" agreed Carly.

And on that note everyone agreed that it was time for bed and sweet dreams of friendly Nessie, the best player of Hide and Seek ever.

A WEE TRIP TO

INVERNESS CALEDONIAN THISTLE FC

It was Saturday morning and Mr J was telling Barra and Carly that he was going to the Caley Thistle v Celtic football match this afternoon with his friends.

"Can we come too, please, please, pretty please?" asked Barra and Carly. We have never, ever been to a football match before. We will be really good, we promise."

"Of course you can," said Mr J, "it will be an exciting game, not many teams manage to win against Celtic." "Maybe it will be Caley Thistle's lucky day" said Barra hopefully. "Carly and I can be their lucky mascots." "What a great idea," said Mr J, "let's hope that will do the trick."

Barra, Carly and Mr J settled down to watch Soccer am to get themselves in the mood for the match. "This is such a funny programme" said Carly" I do like that Mr Rocket and Frankie Fryer, although Mr Frankie is a little bit bonkers isn't he, Barra." "He certainly is" said Barra, "but it's great how he goes around the country visiting all the football stadiums. I wonder if he will come up to Inverness one day, that would be really cool, wouldn't it Mr J." "It sure would, we might even get on the telly box, Barra" said Mr J.

Barra jumped up and did a brilliant impression of Mr Frankie pretending he was at Caley Thistle's stadium.

"Ooh, I do like playing away!" he shouted and Carly and Mr J fell about roaring and laughing. "Oh Barra," giggled Carly, "that was so funny."

Barra, Carly and Mr J were now in brilliant form and ready for the match. They set off and when they arrived at the stadium, Sam, the lovely lady who welcomes everybody, saw them arriving and called them over.

"Hello Mr J, so this is Barra and Carly, I've heard a lot about you two," said Sam. "How would you like to be our lucky mascots today?"

Barra and Carly jumped up and down "Oh yes please, this is the first time we have ever been to a football match, that would be so exciting. I do hope we bring the team lots and lots of luck."

Sam took Barra, Carly and Mr J to meet all the players in the dressing room. Mr Yogi, the Manager, came to say hello "I do hope you have brought a lot of luck with you today, Barra and Carly, we will certainly need it." said Mr Yogi. "We will do our very best" said Barra and then Barra and Carly ran out on to the pitch with the team to warm up. "I have a good feeling about this match" said Barra "I think Caley Thistle will win today". "I think so too" said Carly.

Barra and Carly had great fun running about on the pitch. "Mr Tommy has got the pitch in tip top condition for today's match" said Barra, "it's just as good as Wembley grass. I wish the grass in our back garden was like this."

Barra and Carly took their seats and waited for the kick-off. There was a huge crowd today and Barra said "Mr J what a lot of fans, Caley Thistle have, I've never seen so many people altogether in one place." "Caley Thistle have fans all over the world Barra, even in America and New Zealand, they are very famous, you know" said Mr J. "Wow, that's amazing" said Barra and Carly together. "Mr J, do you think Mr Yogi is related to our cousin Yogi that lives in Yellowstone Park in America?" asked Barra. "That could be why Caley Thistle have fans in America." Mr J laughed and said "He may well be Barra, you never know."

The teams ran out of the tunnel on to the pitch, shook hands and took their places. The referee blew his whistle and the match was underway.

It was end to end football, both teams were playing exceptionally well, it was such an exciting game. "Come on Caley Thistle" shouted Barra and Carly and at 44 minutes Caley Thistle scored. "Hurrah!" cheered the crowd as "He scores when he wants, goal from Billy Mackay!" was announced over the tannoy. The supporters clapped and cheered loudly as the team came off the pitch at half-time.

"Let's sample the Caley Thistle pies" said Mr J, as Sam brought out a large tray of pies to the special guests in the Directors' seats. "Mmm, these are very tasty" said Barra. "Yes, they certainly are" said Carly, "a nice change from cakes."

The referee blew his whistle to start the second half and both teams fought hard for possession of the ball. The second half was just as exciting as the first with both teams trying so hard to score another goal. It was getting close to full-time. "I do hope Celtic don't steal a last minute goal, that last shot on goal was pretty close" said Mr J. It was now into the last couple of minutes of extra time. "I'm so nervous, I can't watch anymore" said Carly, covering her eyes.

"Come on Caley Thistle" shouted Barra and with that Mr Nick tucked the ball, right into the corner of Celtic's net. A huge cheer went up from the crowd and Carly whispered "can I open my eyes now Barra?" "You didn't miss Mr Nick's goal Carly, did you?" "I'm afraid I did" said Carly, "I was too scared to watch in case Celtic scored."

The referee blew the whistle for full-time and everybody jumped up and down cheering Caley Thistle. "Excellent result, 3 points to Caley Thistle" said Mr J. "Yes, it sure was," said Barra "and Mr Dean managed to keep a clean sheet as well, that was just brill!"

The Caley Thistle team were given a standing ovation as they came of the pitch. "Well done boys!" shouted the crowd.

"My paws are sore with clapping so much" said Carly, "I so enjoyed the match." "Me too" croaked Barra, "I'm losing my voice with all that shouting and cheering."

"Do you remember that excellent headline in the newspaper when Caley Thistle knocked Celtic out of the Scottish Cup a few years ago Barra?" asked Mr J. "What was it again, SUPERCALEY GO BALLISTIC, CELTIC ARE ATROCIOUS?   We could make up a new one for today SUPERCARLY BARRA MASCOTS, CELTIC ARE ATROCIOUS.   What do you think?" They all laughed, so pleased that it had been a good day for Caley Thistle and off they went to catch the bus home.

When they arrived home they told the bears all about the exciting match and how they had been chosen to be mascots. "We were very lucky mascots for the team, weren't we?" said Carly" "We certainly were" said Barra.

They showed the bears a picture of them with Mr Nick, who scored one of the goals, and Mr Dean, the goalkeeper.
"You were so lucky Barra and Carly to be mascots" said the bears enviously.   "You do have such an exciting life".   "We certainly do," whispered Barra " but I think I need to rest my voice now."
"Time for bed then," said Carly "that was the best day ever. Goodnight everyone."   Soon Barra and Carly were fast asleep, dreaming of being famous football stars and playing in the World Cup.

A WEE TRIP TO ANTFIELD FARM

It was another lovely day and Barra and Carly were watching the sheep and cows out of the sun room window in the field at the bottom of the garden. It had made them think about their cousin, Lachie the Sheepdog, who looked after Farmer Finlay's sheep over at Antfield Farm.

"Barra, would you like to go and visit Lachie today up at Farmer Finlay's, we haven't seen him for a long time" said Carly.

"What a fantastic idea, Carly," I do like to go to Farmer Finlay's, I love getting a ride on the tractor and seeing the Highland Cows and the sheep.

"Come on then Carly, get yourself ready and we'll get going."

Barra and Carly set off to catch the bus to Antfield Farm. It was only a few miles away at the other side of town so the journey didn't take too long.

They arrived at the farmhouse to the aroma of freshly baked bread. Farmer Annie was a wonderful chef and was always baking when she wasn't looking after the animals. Farmer Annie worked very hard, a lot harder than Farmer Finlay, he just did the bossing about!

"Good morning, Farmer Annie" said Barra and Carly in unison.

"Good morning to you Barra and Carly" said Farmer Annie, "it's lovely to see you both. I've just made a fresh batch of bread. Would you like a piece with my home made strawberry jam?" "Oh yes please, that would be lovely" said Barra. "Thank you so much" said Carly "you are so kind Farmer Annie."

"I'll make an extra piece and you can take it up to the field for Lachie. He has been out looking after the sheep since 6.00 am and he will be needing a wee snack."

Barra and Carly headed up to the field and they soon spotted Lachie. He stopped to enjoy his jammy piece and they had a good blether about all the adventures they had been up to since they had last seen him. "You are always so busy you two" said Lachie, "you have such an exciting life."

"You should come on one of our adventures with us" said Barra. "Och no" said Lachie, "I'm perfectly happy here on the farm, I love looking after the sheep, we have just as much fun here. We get up to lots of mischief when Farmer Finlay isn't looking and we are quite good at playing tricks on him. We move things about when he's not there and then he can't find them. It's really funny watching him playing hide and seek trying to find things, we do have such a laugh."

Barra and Carly waved goodbye to Lachie and went back to the Farmhouse to say cheerio to Farmer Annie. "Thanks for the jammy pieces," said Carly, "that was the best bread and jam I have ever tasted." "You are very welcome" said Farmer Annie "do come and visit again soon, Lachie and I are always so pleased to see you." "We will" said Barra and off they set to the bus stop.

Antfield Farm was just a mile or so from Dores so they decided they would also go along to see the Nessie Man who had a caravan at the shores of Loch Ness. The Nessie Man spent all his time looking for Nessie so Barra and Carly wanted to tell him how lucky they had been to see Nessie when they were on their Nessie Cruise.

They jumped on the bus and a few minutes later they arrived at Dores. They knocked on the Nessie Man's door and when he opened the door they introduced themselves.

"Good afternoon Mr Nessie Man, I am Barra Bear and this is my best friend, Carly Cat. We know that you are always searching for Nessie and we wanted to tell you that we were on a Nessie Cruise a few days ago and we saw Nessie out in the middle of Loch Ness."

"Have you seen Nessie yet?" asked Carly.   "I'm afraid I haven't, I have been looking for years and I have still not spotted her" said the Nessie Man.

"You are so very lucky to have seen her"   "Yes, we know we are very special to have seen her and we will never forget that day, it was so exciting" said Barra.   "Keep looking, though," said Carly, "I'm sure your day will come soon."   "I certainly will" said the Nessie Man.

Barra and Carly waved goodbye to the Nessie Man "Good Luck!" they shouted, and they set off to catch the bus home to Balloch.

When they arrived home they told the bears that Lachie was very well and still working hard looking after the sheep.   Lachie had asked Barra and Carly to say hello to the bears from him and to tell them that he would come and visit them one day soon.

Barra and Carly had taken a selfie of themselves with Lachie and his sheep and they showed the picture to the bears. They all agreed that the picture had turned out rather well.

"Lachie is such a good sheepdog", said Barra, "his sheep all looked so happy, they must love him a lot."

Visiting Lachie today had made Barra and Carly think that it was about time they travelled further afield on their adventures to visit their other cousins who were scattered throughout Scotland. There were so many places they could go, Dunfermline, Dundee, St Andrews, Monifieth, Kinross, Skye, Arran, Mull and lots and lots more. They agreed that they would have to plan an itinerary and get themselves organized.

"I think that's a job for another day, Barra" said Carly, sleepily, and dreaming of all the places that they were going to visit, they both fell fast asleep.

We hope you enjoyed our little stories

Barra and Carly xxx